Twelve at Christmas

~ Twelve short stories for the festive season ~

by Christoffer Petersen & Isabella Muir

TWELVE AT CHRISTMAS

Published in Great Britain
By Outset Publishing Ltd

Published December 2019

ISBN: 978-1-872889-26-9

www.christoffer-petersen.com
www.isabellamuir.com

Cover photo: by Joanna Kosinska (Unsplash)
Cover design: by Christoffer Petersen

Introduction

It all started with an interview. For our first student assignment, we were tasked with interviewing one another to discover our writing goals and ambitions. The internet connection between Greenland and Sussex was intermittent and subject to Arctic interference, but from that day onwards, we have formed a writing bond that has continued to go from strength to strength, through many time zones during our studies, to our first face-to-face meeting at graduation, and beyond.

With a shared love of reading and writing, together with a Master of Arts in Professional Writing from Falmouth University, we continue to work closely to support each other's writing career, swapping skills and experience and developing new ideas and ways to collaborate.

The book you are holding in your hands, or reading on your electronic device, was inspired by the lyrics of the popular Christmas song *The Twelve Days of Christmas*. Working on this anthology has offered us a chance to delve deeper into aspects of many of the characters from our novels and series. Each story has one or more festive elements wrapped around a tale that fits into the existing timelines from our novels and novellas -

sometimes preceding them and sometimes panning out many years into the future. It is the first of our collaborations - hopefully the first of many.

We hope you enjoy the stories as much as we enjoyed writing them. And, if you'd like to know more about our work and our characters, be sure to get your free book and sign up for our newsletters, via the links at the end of this book.

Wishing you all the best for the Holiday Season.

Christoffer and Isabella
November 2019

The first day of Christmas

~ A partridge in a pear tree ~

In which we meet retired police constable David Maratse from *Seven Graves, One Winter*, the first novel in Christoffer Petersen's Greenland Crime series.

One partridge, one tree

~ Inussuk, Greenland, 2021 ~

The bright bulbs shone through the paper Christmas stars hanging in the windows of the houses of Inussuk. Blues and reds lit the snow in a soft glow, as retired police constable David Maratse fiddled with the chains that tethered his team to the beach beside the frozen sea. He gripped the lead dog, Tinka, between his legs and prised the flat end of the screwdriver into the metal clasp attaching the chain to her collar. Tinka wriggled between his knees, squirming in the light from Maratse's headtorch. His breath mingled with Tinka's, pearling between the thick hairs of her fur and freezing on the wisp of a beard that Maratse wore in a goatee, something new for the winter.

'*Tassa*,' Maratse said, as he fiddled with the clasp.

'She wants to play,' said sergeant Petra Jensen, as she clomped through the snow in oversized winter boots. She hugged a thick fleece to her chest, tucking her bare hands under her arms. A thin rime of frost started to build on the tips of her long black hair.

'She can play when we get back.'

'Did you hear that, Tinka?' Petra said, as she knelt in the snow in front of the lead dog. 'We can play when you get back from town.'

'She can,' Maratse said. 'You promised to cook.'

'And you'll decorate the tree.'

'*Iiji,*' he said, smiling as the clasp finally opened. He tucked it into his pocket and then put Tinka into harness. Petra walked beside Maratse as he took Tinka to the head of the team and clipped her into the ganglines. The smaller dogs started to whine, while one of the larger dogs closest to the tips of the sledge runners, jumped up and down, raring to go.

'They're excited,' Petra said, curling her fingers into Maratse's.

'Hmm.'

'It's the Christmas spirit,' she said. 'They're obviously infected.'

'*Iiji.*'

'It must work faster on dogs.' Petra tugged Maratse's hand as she kissed him on his cheek. 'I'm going back inside,' she said. 'Don't forget the duck.'

Maratse nodded as Petra let go of his hand. He watched her walk back to the house, waited until she turned to wave from the deck, before making the sledge ready for the run to Uummannaq. He gave the command for Tinka to lead the dogs down to the ice the second Petra stepped inside their house.

The first stretch of sea ice from Inussuk along the coast to Qaarsut was smooth. Maratse avoided the ice closest to the shore, aware that the current chewed at the underside of the ice. It was too thin for a snowmobile already, and Maratse wouldn't take the risk with the dogs. His neighbour, Karl, had given him the latest update on the ice the night before. Maratse could still remember the smell of Buuti's narwhal stew that she had served. Petra had praised it too but had eaten far less than Buuti wanted her to.

'Keeping your slim figure might be fine for Nuuk,' Buuti had said. 'But you need more layers to get through the winter in Inussuk, and Maratse's jacket doesn't count,' she added, before Petra could respond.

The bond between the two women had grown over a short period of time, with Buuti assuming responsibility for Petra's physical and mental wellbeing. She left the romance to Maratse but couldn't help nudging him in the right direction when she felt he needed it. Karl had quietly told her to stop, but Petra was all for it, suggesting that any help would be appreciated. While the gentle jibes and teasing often drifted around Maratse, he had begun to appreciate what could be described as an awakening. Karl told him it could be love.

But it wasn't love that drove Maratse across the ice in temperatures that fell far below minus twenty degrees. Keeping him indoors was the hard part, unless he had a good book to occupy him. But Petra had insisted that *this* Christmas would be different. She was feeling better than she had felt in a long time. Her job was going well, and the commissioner had hinted, more than once, about a promotion, and that she should take some time over Christmas to think about it.

'It would mean even less time in Inussuk,' she said once they finished eating Buuti's narwhal stew. 'But better pay, so I could afford the flights, maybe once a month.'

Maratse remembered Karl kicking him under the table, provoking more than just a grunt from the retired constable.

He thought about it some more as the runners grated across the ice towards Uummannaq. Petra had suggested he move to Nuuk, knowing that he would struggle, but that it was a possibility, at least. Maratse wasn't so sure, and they had decided to wait until after Christmas before talking about it again.

Maratse chose to focus on the kiss instead, smiling at the memory of Petra's warm lips on his cold cheek. They would find a way to make it work, just like the dogs found a way around the patches of thin ice beneath drifts of snow in the frozen harbour of Uummannaq. Maratse drove them up and over the ice ramp, as close as he could get to the store before stopping the sledge and tethering the dogs to the loop of an old buoy frozen by the side of the road.

He picked the tree up first, presenting his ticket at the checkout, and then agreeing to meet around the back of the store. The trees had arrived on one of the last supply boats a few months earlier. It was Buuti who reminded Maratse to reserve one of the trees. She had sent Karl and Maratse into town in a small fibreglass dinghy the day the ship had arrived, together with a list of things they must buy that day, even if they had to wait until the evening.

Maratse remembered being impressed by her urgency, whereas Karl merely shrugged.

'It's always like this,' he had said, as they pushed the boat into the water.

Maratse finally understood when the store assistant met him at the back of the store. There was only one tree left.

'You're lucky,' the assistant said. 'They only delivered half of what they promised this year.'

'Hmm,' Maratse said.

'Are you buying anything else?'

'Why?'

'I just thought you might want to wait before putting the tree on the sledge. It would be a shame to lose it.'

'*Iiji.*' Maratse left the tree where it was and followed the assistant back inside.

The section of the freezer that contained poultry was almost empty, and all the duck breasts were gone. Maratse chose one of the two birds remaining – two breasts in a vacuum-packed bag.

'That's not duck,' said a woman standing beside Maratse.

'What is it?'

'Partridge.'

'Hmm,' Maratse said. He thought about Petra and her Christmas spirit. 'Does it taste like duck?'

'*Imaqa,*' the woman said. 'Maybe.'

Maratse dropped the frozen partridge breasts into his shopping basket, adding a few packets of sweets and chocolates on his way to the checkout. He tucked everything into the pockets of his much worn and well-loved police jacket, before climbing the stairs to the first floor. He picked up his order from the jewellery section, thanking the assistant as he tucked the tiny envelope into his inside pocket. Maratse allowed himself a half smile at the thought of how Petra might react and what Buuti might say when they realised he had been listening, that he could in fact be romantic when the occasion called for it. One could even say he had been infected by the Christmas spirit.

The spirit vanished less than thirty minutes after Maratse sledged out of Uummannaq, when the driver of a large dog team tried to pass Maratse from behind. Instead of driving the dogs to the right of Maratse, the chasing team split down the middle and enveloped him. Maratse's smaller sledge and smaller team was engulfed in a blur of lines and teeth and fur. The sledge behind drove up and over the uprights of Maratse's sledge, causing him to duck and roll onto the ice. The frozen partridge fell out of his pocket and skittered along the ice just out of reach. The driver of the larger sledge, trapped between the ganglines of both his dogs and Maratse's, started to cut the lines, freeing the dogs and allowing both men to recover their sledges. Tinka raced across the ice, beyond Maratse's reach and influence.

'I'm sorry,' said the dog driver. 'They're not my dogs.'

'Hmm,' Maratse said, as he called his own team to him, tying new knots before attaching the shorter lines to the front of his sledge.

'Is that your tree?'

Maratse looked in the direction the dog driver was pointing and sighed. The top of the tree was broken in the collision and a swathe of needles darkened the ice.

'Hmm,' he said. Maratse picked up his tree and tied it onto his sledge. When the driver pulled away with his team, Maratse called for Tinka to come. He felt his shoulders relax when he spotted her on the ice only a few sledge lengths away. 'Tinka,' he said. 'Come.'

Tinka took her time, and her strange gait made Maratse frown. He worried that she might have broken a leg when the sledge ran into them. The closest veterinarian was in Ilulissat, too far away for a house call. Even Maratse couldn't fix a broken leg, and he felt his hand move involuntarily towards his hip where he once wore his service pistol. He let his hand fall to his side when he realised there was nothing wrong with her legs, but something was stuck between her teeth, blocking her airway.

He caught Tinka by the collar, pinched her jaws open with his finger and thumb, and then stuck his free hand inside her mouth. He shook his head as his fingers gripped the wet plastic wrapper that used to contain two partridge breasts.

'At least it wasn't duck,' he said, as he tugged the rest of the plastic out of Tinka's mouth. He stuffed the plastic into his pocket before tying a new knot in Tinka's line and adding her to the team.

Maratse wished he had a cigarette as they sledged the last few kilometres back to Inussuk. He looked at the tree, almost laughed at the bare and broken branches, and then remembered the envelope in his pocket. He unzipped his jacket and pressed his fingers inside the pocket until they caught the edge of the envelope. He let out a long sigh and then leaned back against the sledge bag. Maratse fished a packet of sweets out of his pocket, deciding that he was in enough trouble already, and that a few sweets wouldn't be missed.

He finished the packet before they reached Inussuk.

Maratse took longer than usual to sort out the dogs on the beach. Karl waved to him from the deck of his house, only to frown in the light of the Christmas star as Maratse carried the broken tree up the steps to his front door.

'What's that?' Karl asked.

'The tree.'

'Not much of a tree.'

Maratse shrugged. 'It was the last one.'

Karl finished his cigarette and walked over. 'But you remembered the duck?' he said, as he reached the bottom step.

'It was a partridge.'

'What's a partridge?'

'Ask Tinka,' Maratse said, with a nod towards the dogs.

'Well, good luck,' Karl said. He strolled back to his house as Petra opened the door.

Maratse leaned the tree against the wooden railings that ran around the deck.

'Tree,' he said, and pointed at it.

'Okay,' Petra said.

Maratse pulled the chewed plastic wrapper from his pocket, holding it up for a second for Petra to see before dumping it in the rubbish bin.

'And that was the duck?' Petra asked.

'*Eeqqi*,' Maratse said. 'That was the partridge.'

'Right.' Petra crossed her arms over her chest, and said, 'Did you manage to bring anything back in one piece?'

'Just this,' Maratse said, as he reached into his jacket. 'Hold out your hand.'

Petra uncurled her arm from her body and spread her palm in front of Maratse. He placed the envelope flat on her palm and smiled.

'What's this?' she asked, as she opened the envelope.

'Christmas spirit,' he said. 'For this year, and all the rest that follow. Until I die.'

'Until you die?'

'*Iiji*,' he said.

Petra pulled a simple gold ring out of the envelope and into the light from the Christmas stars. She pinched it between her finger and thumb, pressing it to her lips as she looked at Maratse. Her eyes glistened, and the first tear to trickle down her cheek cooled in the crisp Greenland air.

'Yes,' she said, as she pulled Maratse close.

'I haven't asked you anything.'

'Not yet,' Petra said, as she pulled him inside the house.

THE END

The second day of Christmas

~ Two turtle doves ~

In which we meet Michelle Juke, the daughter of Janie and Greg Juke. Michelle is just a baby when we first meet her in *The Invisible Case*, the third novel from Isabella Muir's Sussex Crime series, set in 1960s England.

Turtles and doves

~ Sussex, England, 1975 ~

Joshua was having a tantrum. The rest of the class watched, many of them giggling. At least the girls were giggling, while the boys made a point of moving away from Joshua, thereby avoiding his flailing arms and legs.

It was as Miss Padstow announced the parts for the play that the trouble had started.

'Lucy Riley, you will be the Angel Gabriel.'

'Yes miss.' Lucy flicked back her blonde hair and stood a little straighter, holding her arms out to simulate angel's wings.

'Mark Rees will be Joseph and Annette Tour will be Mary.'

She continued allocating children to roles. Once each of the characters of the nativity play had been selected, it was time to choose the animals.

'Michelle Juke, you will be a dove.'

'A dove, miss?'

'You have a good singing voice and you will need to "coo".'

'Yes miss.' Michelle started to *coo* quietly, testing herself to discover whether it was best to *coo* as high as her voice would allow, or if it was easier and more impressive to use a deep tone. She had to stop her practising when all the *cooing* made her throat tickle, resulting in an attack of coughing.

'Fetch some water, Michelle.' Miss Padstow pointed to the sink in the corner of the classroom that was usually only used when they had to wash their hands after playing with plasticine.

By that time Joshua had calmed a little.

'Now, Joshua, what was that all about?' Miss Padstow used a calming tone. It wasn't the first time Joshua had had a tantrum. The last time was when the new dinner lady, Mrs Mellor, had told him off for not eating his peas.

'Vegetables are good for you, they will make you grow big and strong, just like your dad,' she told him, before having to duck quickly. His response to her advice was to take one of his shoes off and hurl it at her. Luckily he missed. Mrs Mellor didn't know about Joshua and later when she found out she felt sorry for what she had said.

'I want to be Joseph,' Joshua announced. 'It's his job to look after the baby. I have to help the Virgin Mary while she is on the donkey and then I'm to knock on all the doors even though they will turn us away.'

'Well done, Joshua. You have learned the story of the nativity really well. But, remember, that once Mary's baby was born, it wasn't just Joseph who looked after him.'

Joshua knew about the three wise men and all the presents they brought. Each year, Joshua went along with the other children from the home to a Christmas party, where they could choose from a pile of second-hand toys that had been donated. It seemed that some children had too much of everything and some had almost nothing.

The rest of the class had stopped listening to the conversation between Joshua and Miss Padstow because Robert Marsh was giving out the milk. He had been given the job of milk monitor for the week. The others queued up as he handed them a bottle each, first putting a straw into the top. That was his favourite part of the job. If he pushed the straw right into the middle of the silver foil top it made a kind of sucking sound. He'd discovered that he could almost make a tune with it, which made him think his dad was right. Robert's dad could play music using just about anything, even the washboard his mum used to use. And his dad could whistle, although now that Robert's mum had gone the whistling and the music had stopped.

As the rest of the class filed past him, clutching their bottles of milk, Robert tried to make a whistling sound to match the popping of the bottle tops. But once Miss Padstow and Joshua had finished their conversation he had to stop his whistling. He would practise some more later, on his way home. Then when his dad got in from work he would show him just how well he could do it and that would make his dad smile.

The nativity play was to be performed on the final day of term. The class had been practising and Miss Padstow had said she was very proud of them all. There had been a few difficult moments when the donkey stood backwards and trod heavily on the chicken's foot. Alison Lacey was the chicken and being the smallest girl in the class she also had the smallest feet, which made it surprising that John Brown (who was the donkey) had managed to trample on her. Alison had screeched, in fact the noise she made was very similar to the noise of a chicken. But Miss Padstow intervened and made John apologise and the next time they practised that part of the play when all the animals filed past the crib to welcome the baby Jesus, everyone made sure to keep well away from each other.

Straight after lunch on the day of the play the children began to get into their costumes. Parents started arriving at 2pm, taking their seats ready for the start of the performance.

Michelle's mum, Janie, had spent several evenings making her costume. As a dove, she had to be dressed all in white and Janie was a little worried that her daughter would look more like a ghost than a dove, but she showed her how to hold her arms out as though they were the wings of a bird. Whenever Janie was helping to lay the table or do the drying up, she practised her *cooing*. Each time they visited her granddad, Philip, she would test it out on him. Janie had explained that her Granddad was the perfect person to comment, on account of him being blind, which somehow made his hearing even sharper.

All the performers had to wait in Class 3 while Miss Padstow kept a check on the school hall, waiting until everyone had arrived. There were so many parents and friends in the audience that some people had to stand.

'Have you seen my mum and dad, miss? Have they arrived yet?' was a repeated refrain from many of the children each time Miss Padstow returned to the classroom.

Joshua didn't ask about his mum or dad, because he had never met them. He had been in

Dr Barnardo's children's home since he was a baby. He knew that some of the staff from the home would be there in the audience because they had promised him, but it wasn't the same as having a dad there. Just like being a turtle wasn't as good as being Joseph.

'Are you all ready children? Don't forget to smile.' Miss Padstow led them from the classroom to the side of the stage set out at the front of the school hall. Several of the children who were in animal costumes struggled to walk without tripping over, but soon they were lined up and keen to get started.

Joshua shuffled forward. The cardboard shell that was strapped to his back felt awkward, parts of it sticking into his shoulders and the backs of his legs. He practised his lines under his breath, making sure he remembered each word, before stepping onto the stage.

'Welcome ladies and gentlemen to St Wilfrid's nativity play and thank you for coming. I am a turtle.'

Miss Padstow had explained to Joshua how important it was to be a turtle. She gave a small cough from the sidelines, reminding Joshua that there was still more he had to say.

He turned around to show the audience the shell on his back. 'The baby Jesus didn't just have Mary and Joseph looking after him, he had the angels and the three wise men and sheep, donkeys, chickens and doves.'

As Joshua mentioned each of the animals, they filed onto the stage. When Michelle saw her mum, dad and granddad she attempted a wave, but her hands were hidden inside the wings of her dove costume. Some of the other animals also tried to wave, with a similar result.

Then Robert, who was a shepherd, came to stand beside Joshua and started to whistle. And as he did, his dad, who had been sitting right at the back of the audience (almost as if he was hiding), stood up and walked towards the stage. He whistled along with Robert and soon several of the men in the audience stood and began to whistle. Then it was as though Joseph and Mary and the baby Jesus and the knocking on the doors and being turned away and the coldness of the stable, even the presents from the wise men - none of these things were as important as the whistling.

That was when Joshua knew that Miss Padstow was right all along. It didn't matter if you were Joseph or if you were a turtle. Even if a dad was all you had, or even if you didn't have a dad at all, there was never just one person looking out for you.

At the end of the play all the characters took a bow, but it was the turtle who got the loudest cheer.

THE END

The third day of Christmas

~ Three French hens ~

In which we meet Konstabel Fenna Brongaard from *The Ice Star*, the first novel in Christoffer Petersen's Greenland Trilogy of military thrillers.

The Frenchman

~ Toronto, Canada, 2022 ~

It was her favourite pub in Toronto and had the right balance of style and comfort, depending upon who you talked to. You could dress casually but be comfortable alongside suits from the city, without looking out of place. What's more you could enjoy a plate of fat British-style chips with a greasy burger and a pint, something Konstabel Fenna Brongaard appreciated as she waited for the Frenchman.

Fenna had a good view of the door and additional exits from her seat in the corner. She hid her observations between bites of burger, avoiding eye contact with the single men propping up the bar, and feigning sufficient interest in her smartphone, as young women of her age tended to do. She scrolled through an Instagram gallery with one finger, while dipping fat chips in ketchup, playing the role of the single woman grabbing a quick bite to eat at the end of the day, before braving the snow on the way home. The *quick bite* had developed into an early evening meal as the Frenchman failed to appear. Fenna made her burger last with another pint of English beer. The condensation on the side of the beer glass glittered with the Christmas lights draped around the bar and corners of the pub.

'Do you mind if I join you?'

Fenna looked up as one of the braver single men from the bar approached her table. She had seen him approach but chose not to notice until he was at the table. It was just possible that it was him playing the role of a city trader, pretending to be lonely at Christmas, until he was satisfied that Fenna was alone. The truth was just that, she was alone, without backup. Meredith, Fenna's controller with CSIS, the Canadian Security Intelligence Service, had argued against her meeting the Frenchman without backup. So Fenna played the trust card, implying that Meredith needed to show a deeper level of trust than she had up to that point.

'I don't trust you, Konstabel,' Meredith had said. 'I'm not sure I ever will. But regardless of that, I'm still responsible for you. You've proved useful so far, I don't want this to be your last Christmas in the service.'

Meredith's lack of trust in Fenna, however, was eclipsed by what she knew of the Frenchman, an elusive secret agent, of supposedly Canadian origin, who claimed to have information about a mole in the CSIS. The Frenchman's reputation for being difficult to trace added a certain weight to his claim, forcing Meredith to give in to his conditions and allow Fenna to meet him alone, without backup. But Meredith chose the time and place of the meet, suggesting that it was highly unlikely that anything would happen in a traders' pub in the heart of Toronto. After a quick appraisal of the man hovering beside her table, Fenna had to agree that her boss might be right.

'I'm waiting for someone,' she said, and turned back to her smartphone. The man waited a second longer than Fenna expected, before returning to the bar. He shot her one more glance before ordering another drink. Fenna decided she would leave before he finished it, unless the Frenchman turned up before then.

It was the woman's perfume that caught Fenna's attention as the pub door opened and a young woman walked in. Strong enough to turn the men's heads at the bar, the scent reminded Fenna of the women on *The Ice Star*, a luxury adventure cruise ship she had had the misfortune of encountering early in her military career. In fact, her experience on board that ship had cut short her military career and thrust her into the murky world of espionage and counterintelligence. So it came as no surprise when the woman, all six feet of her, walked directly to her table, pulled out a chair opposite Fenna and sat down.

'You've been waiting for me,' the woman said. She glanced at Fenna's plate and the two pint glasses, and added, 'For a little while, I can see.'

'You're mistaking me for someone else,' Fenna said.

'I don't think so.'

The woman unzipped the tight leather jacket she wore above her figure-hugging trousers. She unwound the shemagh scarf she wore around her neck and piled it on the table next to Fenna's plate. The woman glistened as the snowflakes in her hair melted. She leaned her elbows on the table and studied Fenna.

'A hoodie and jeans,' she said. 'Just as I expected. But you know, with that face,' the woman traced a circle in the air between them, 'and your hair... you really could do more with your looks.'

Fenna took a sip of beer as the woman continued.

'We do have some photos of you in our file, from when you attended balls and high society functions.' She smiled. 'You clean up very well, Konstabel. So I imagine all this is just you being undercover?'

Fenna put her glass down slowly. She looked around the woman, scanning the bar, trying to spot her backup team before wondering if, or more likely *when*, she would have to react. She could easily draw the tiny Glock 42 subcompact pistol she wore around her ankle if she crossed one leg over the other, but the woman had obviously considered that; Fenna could feel her feet pressing against the outside of Fenna's boots. Fenna's file clearly contained a lot of detailed information. *Too much*, she thought, as she leaned back in her seat.

'All right,' Fenna said. 'Let's talk.'

'We are talking.'

'About the Frenchman.'

'*Oui*, of course,' the woman said, and smiled. One of her front teeth, Fenna noticed was crooked and a little of the woman's expensive lipstick had caught in the overlap. 'Do continue, Konstabel.'

Fenna brushed a loose strand of her hair to one side, as she decided what approach she should take. There was still no sign of any backup team. Either there wasn't one, or they were very good.

'You're either working for him, or you *are* him.'

'But you can't decide which, can you? Or,' the woman said, 'you're just hoping it's one of those two options, because you don't like the third, do you?'

'The third?'

'The one where I've intercepted the Frenchman, gutted him for information, as only I can do, and discovered the details of your meeting.'

'It's possible,' Fenna said. So possible that she had to fight the urge to flick the table towards the woman, pull the Glock from her ankle holster and put two bullets in her chest. Fenna took another sip of beer instead, while the woman ordered a Martini.

'This is the fun part of our job,' she said, once the barman had brought her drink. She left a smear of lipstick on the glass as she took her first sip. 'We get to play our roles, each of us trying to outsmart and outguess the other. Who will win, I wonder? The chic and sophisticated, possibly American, probably Canadian, young and talented intelligence agent, or the curiously brutal ex-Special Forces operative, currently slumming it with the Canadian Security Intelligence Service?' The woman took another sip of Martini. 'By the way, how is Meredith?'

Fenna smiled as the barman selected a Christmas playlist from the pub's streaming service, eliciting groans and gentle complaints from the men sitting around the bar as the first few bars of Wham!'s *Last Christmas* tumbled out of the speakers.

'Meredith is fine,' Fenna said. 'And she sends her regards.'

'Really? How interesting.'

Fenna waited for the woman to say something more, but a faint vibration of the phone Fenna guessed was in a pocket inside her jacket distracted her.

'A reminder?' Fenna said, as the woman looked up.

'I do have somewhere else to be.' The woman leaned over the table to whisper, 'This isn't really my kind of place.'

'I know,' Fenna said.

'You do?'

'Yes,' she said. 'The Frenchman told me.'

It was the woman's turn to pause. Fenna watched as she ran through the same calculations that had occupied Fenna only minutes earlier. From what she knew of Claudette Beauchêne, the forty-year old favoured a Beretta pistol, despite it ruining the cut of her jacket. The absence of a bulge at her hips and ribs confirmed what Fenna believed to be true, there was a backup team, and they would be waiting outside. The Frenchman had laid a trap, and it was time to spring it.

'We could go outside,' Fenna said, as Claudette recovered her composure. 'If that would make you more comfortable?'

'Could we?' Claudette pushed back her chair. 'That's very sweet of you.' She pulled a twenty-dollar note from her pocket and pressed it onto the table with her finger. 'I assume you've paid already?'

'I'm good to go,' Fenna said. She slid along the bench until she was clear of the table and stood up.

'It's a shame really,' Claudette said. 'Under different circumstances…'

'We could have been two girlfriends enjoying a Christmas drink?'

'*Oui*, something like that.'

Fenna nodded at the door, slipped her phone into her pocket, and said, 'Another time, perhaps?'

'Another time then,' Claudette said.

Claudette picked up her shemagh and zipped her jacket. Fenna noted that she carried the shemagh in her hand, rather than wrapping it around her neck. Either Claudette was concerned that Fenna might strangle her with it, or she intended to use it on Fenna. Fenna decided she would have done the same, carry it in her hand until they reached the door, and then try to twist it around her enemy's neck as soon as they walked out of the pub. The snow swirling down the street would provide a suitable distraction, and most of the pedestrians walking past the Flatiron pub would be walking face-down into the wind, wishing they had taken a taxi, too cold to notice two young women staggering out of a pub.

Fenna needn't have worried, Claudette was clearly under orders. She held the door for Fenna and pointed to a van parked on the kerb just a short walk from the pub.

'If you'll get in,' she said. 'No fuss. Then we can just get this all over with.'

'You'll tell me what *this* is, won't you?' Fenna said.

'Of course, as soon as we're inside the van.'

Fenna slowed as they approached the side door of the van. She winked at the driver as Claudette rapped her knuckles on the door.

'Don't flirt with the help,' Claudette said, as the door slid open. 'It'll only break their heart in the end.'

'More than you know,' Fenna said, as she shoved Claudette with her shoulder, just as the two men inside the van pulled her inside. Fenna followed, closing the side door as the driver pulled away from the kerb. It had taken just four seconds from the moment Claudette knocked on the van door to when the driver pulled into traffic.

Claudette fought for a second, until the larger of the two men clamped one hand over her mouth and nose, and the other around her throat. His partner knelt on Claudette's thighs and pinned her arms to her sides. Fenna waited until Claudette's eyes began to bulge before nodding for the man to remove his hand from her mouth.

'I think you must be a Christmas gift from the Frenchman,' Fenna said. 'I thought I was going to meet him. But instead, he sent us you.'

Fenna leaned back against the side of the van to send a text to Meredith. Claudette glared at her when she looked up, but Fenna just smiled. She called out the driver's name, and said, 'Wham! Really?'

'Meredith said you would recognise it.'

'She was right,' Fenna said. She waited until they turned the corner and then closed her eyes. The Frenchman had kept his part of the deal and delivered one hen for Christmas. 'Just two to go,' Fenna whispered, as the men secured Claudette and the driver tuned the radio in search of Christmas songs.

THE END

The fourth day of Christmas

~ Four calling birds ~

In which we meet Zara and Gabrielle from
The Tapestry Bag, the first novel from Isabella
Muir's Sussex Crime series, set in 1960s England.

Four birds

~ Sussex, England, 1967 ~

There's a sense of freedom that comes with Christmas, which is reflected on people's faces. Families who have barely enough to pay for a pound of mince manage to find the money for a little extravagance. Not luxury by many people's standards, but more than is needed. Isn't that a luxury of sorts?

I know men who will open a gift on Christmas morning to find a packet of chocolate biscuits. A gift from their wife, for which they will exclaim, '*Just what I wanted*', and the couple will embrace and laugh at the nonsense of it all.

I know too that our mother won't be wrapping biscuits. She doesn't need to put pennies in a tin each week with the hope that when they are counted out in the middle of December they might stretch to a bag of walnuts, or some tangerines. There are pounds in her purse, not pennies. She can wave her cheque book at the shop assistant, point at the silver cufflinks she has chosen after just a brief time looking in the jeweller's window. Silver cufflinks. Is there anything more worthless than to decorate the edges of a shirt? Perhaps a tiepin would score the same in a list of pointless gifts.

These are the thoughts that are absorbing me the first time I see her. It is the contours of her face that catch my eye. She flicks her hair back, exposing the angled jaw line. It is just a moment and then she is swept up in the midst of all the other Christmas shoppers.

I carry on walking, reach my bedsit and switch on the radio. The first two items on the news present me with a choice. I can mourn the thousands of young men dying in the Vietnam war, or I can prepare myself to mourn those still living who will die when the atom bomb explodes.

While others have been writing Christmas cards, polishing the dishes they use just once a year for the grand Christmas Day feast, I have been marching. Protesting about a world that is changing. Friends have joined me on the march. We link arms and push ahead up a street to see people moving out of our way. It's like a parting of the waves, with those who are nonchalant standing to one side, while we who clamour for our voices to be heard push forward.

One of my fellow marchers is Owen. He has followed me with a persistence that makes me think his focus is not the cause. I shout out to all who will listen, but he has another agenda. It is confirmed when I respond to a knock on my door.

'Zara,' he says, hands in his pockets, hair slicked back with Brylcreem and so much aftershave that I have to stand back. He reaches a hand out to me, instead I put mine up to my face to suppress a sneeze.

'Owen.' I can't think of what else to say. He waits to come in, but I know that once he is inside my bedsit it's as though I've agreed to him being inside my life.

'Are you marching today? I could wait while you get ready. We could go together.' His tone is almost pleading. It makes me feel sad for him.

Immediately I recognise the emotions I have pushed away. Samuel. I'd felt sad for him too. And look how that ended. I have to blame myself, even though the first time I met him all I wanted was to make him smile. The event that would change our lives happened outside Archer's café, which was also where we first met. I was outside and Samuel was inside, the other side of a glass window that represented all the divisions that I now know existed between us. I didn't know back then, or perhaps I chose not to know. Looking back now I can see the irony of that first encounter. Because, of course, in the end it was him on the outside and I who sheltered within the comfort of belonging.

The fight started in an unexpected way and ended with Samuel laying on a stretcher, with his face bleeding, his life torn apart in a way that doctors and nurses could never fix. The four boys were local. I didn't know their names, but I'd seen them around. I'm fairly certain two of them were brothers, as least they looked so much alike that it would be too much of a coincidence if they weren't. The brothers towered over the other two in the gang. I'm calling it a gang, maybe it was, maybe it wasn't. But that day it operated in every way I imagined a gang to behave. The boy with the long black hair appeared to be in charge. The brothers looked to him to make the important decisions about where to hang out, when to leave, even when to speak. He had a way of commanding attention, so when he was about to speak he held his hand up, palm facing the others and they fell silent. It was disturbing to watch, but fascinating too.

The day of the fight the brothers turned up first. They were standing outside Archer's when I arrived. Samuel was already inside. I'd arranged to meet him there straight after school. He'd been set some really tricky history homework and before we left school he'd spoken to me about it. It was about the Norman Conquest, events that led up to the Battle of Hastings. He joked that my mother might know about the Normans, given that she is French. I gave him a playful thump on the arm, told him not to be so cheeky.

'She might be old, but not that old.'

He smiled his brilliant smile, the one that caught my attention the first day I saw him.

'How is it that your teeth are so white?' I had asked him.

'They are not really so white,' he said. 'It's just that my skin is so black.' He laughed a deep belly laugh, that made me laugh too.

But then there was the confrontation. The gang of boys were standing outside the cafe when I arrived. Samuel came out to greet me.

'Trying to chat up the local talent, eh?' the gang leader shouted at Samuel, pushing him, wanting a reaction. I stood between them. A moment later Samuel had moved me to one side and moments after that Samuel was laying on the floor with his beautiful face cut and bleeding.

All this time I've been thinking of Samuel while Owen stands at the door, waiting.

'I'm not marching today,' I say. Then, stupidly, I relent. 'We could go for a coffee, if you like.'

Owen's frown disappears from his forehead, he parts his lips to smile and I stare at his teeth. An ache runs through my body as I am reminded again of Samuel.

Owen links his arm through mine as we walk up the High Street. Several times we have to stand aside as shoppers struggle past, laden with heavy bags and awkward-shaped parcels. A mother pushes through with a pram that has silver tinsel attached to the hood. A man holds a bunch of holly aloft. He is trying to be cautious, to avoid the sharp spikes stabbing someone's eye. Instead, it is as though he is using the holly in place of mistletoe, hoping to catch a Christmas kiss from a passer-by.

I look up towards the holly and look down at the heads of the shoppers and it's then that I see her again. This time I see the back of her head as she scurries off down a side street.

It's on the third occasion I see her that I confront her. Owen isn't with me. I've come out with the intention of buying a loaf of bread. This morning I broke up the last piece of crust that I'd left to dry in the breadbin, ready to put out for the birds. As winter takes a grip so the wildlife need a helping hand. Just outside the only window of my bedsit is a low wall. Each day four finches fly down and sit side by side, as though they are preparing to hold a meeting. One arrives first, then sings aloud, calling to the others. When I get back I plan to scatter the breadcrumbs and watch my four calling birds peck each piece until the ground is clean.

I don't reach the bakery, because once I see Gabrielle I sense that something bad is going to happen. She goes into a chemist's shop and I follow. I watch as she sidles up to the counter, picking up first one lipstick, then another. I haven't seen her wear that coat before. If she has enough to buy a Mary Quant design, then she has enough money to pay for the lipstick that I see her slip into her coat pocket.

I can't walk away and yet I want nothing more than to distance myself from my twin sister. The mirror image that I have seen reflected back at me since we were born, just ten minutes apart.

'Gabrielle.' I touch her arm and she pulls away. 'If you are sure that is the lipstick you want, why don't we take it to the counter. I could buy it for you if you like, call it an early Christmas present.'

She dips her hand into her pocket again, retrieving the lipstick and replacing it on the stand.

'Have you been following me?' She doesn't hide her hatred of me and once again I feel sad. We are sisters and yet we will never be friends.

She knows about Samuel. She knows his family had to make the only decision that was left to them, to return to Jamaica, leaving behind the mother country they thought would welcome them with open arms. Instead those arms were raised in anger and prejudice.

I think about the four calling birds and their simple life. And then I think about Owen, Samuel, Gabrielle and me. We will never sit side by side in harmony. Everywhere I look there is imbalance.

I've scattered the breadcrumbs now and will watch the birds peck each piece until the light fades.

THE END

The fifth day of Christmas

~ Five gold rings ~

In which we meet police commissioner Petra 'Piitalaat' Jensen from *The Calendar Man*, the first novel in Christoffer Petersen's Dark Advent series set in Greenland.

Greenland gold

~ Nuuk, Greenland, 2043 ~

It's hard to imagine a Greenland without Constable David Maratse. After so many adventures, living at the very edge of the world, to lose that voice – however little he used it – still seems strange, even two years after his death. So, when police commissioner Petra Jensen invited me for coffee, I jumped at the chance to reminisce about our favourite and most reluctant hero.

'He often mentioned you,' Petra said, as we sat in the bay window of the café. 'And when I heard you were in town…'

'Just passing through.'

'Well, I thought it would be a good opportunity to catch up.'

'Yes,' I said, as the waitress came to take our order. We both chose something plain, simple coffee, as Maratse preferred it.

'I wondered,' Petra said, as the waitress left, 'if you've had time to consider my proposal?'

'The book?' I said, thinking back to Petra's message, in which she presented the idea of collecting Maratse's stories.

'It's just, he touched so many people,' she said, as the waitress returned with our coffee. 'I thought it might be fun to give something back.'

'You want me to ghost write it?'

'No.' Petra shook her head. 'Absolutely not. It has to be you who writes it, your name on the cover.'

'But you want to donate the proceeds to charity.'

'A percentage, perhaps, if you think it will sell?'

'I do,' I said, curious that Petra should have been the first to mention the idea. I had been thinking about it since Maratse's death. Even my editor had called, suggesting that he would forego retirement for the sake of that one project. My stories about Maratse had kept his magazine, *The Narwhal*, going for several years.

'Good,' Petra said. 'But how do we begin?'

'I have my articles and my notes. But it would be good to include a more personal story, something to start the collection.'

'Like an introduction?'

'Yes, but very personal. Something about the two of you, perhaps?'

I had been wanting to ask the commissioner about her relationship with Maratse for years. During our time together his subtle and silent ways had both inspired and infuriated me, in equal parts. But the chance to really get under his skin – and not just his family background, but something more personal – had eluded me.

'About David and me?'

'Yes.'

'I'm not sure…'

I had feared as much, which is probably why I had never mentioned it, never pushed, too scared to drive Petra away and close that particular avenue and opportunity for good.

'Something he wouldn't tell anyone, you mean?'

'Yes,' I said. 'But it doesn't have to be embarrassing, or inappropriate. Just human.'

'Just David?'

'Yes. Just him.'

Petra said nothing more for a few minutes. She sipped her coffee, staring out at the swathes of red and gold decorations lining both sides of the street. The Dutch immigrants in New Amsterdam had embraced the Greenlandic tradition of brightening each dark winter with a wealth of illumination and colour that only the Chinese seemed capable of competing with. Maratse wouldn't have liked it, of course. He would have preferred the natural colours of the Northern Lights, but in a strange way the artificial lights seemed appropriate and I liked them.

'There is something,' Petra said, after a long silence. 'Although it is quite personal.'

'I can be delicate,' I said.

'No, don't be *that*. He needs teasing. It would do him good, remind him that we haven't forgotten him.'

'What is it?' I asked, more than a little intrigued.

'It's about his romantic side.'

'Romantic side? I'm sorry,' I said, stifling a laugh. 'I can't imagine him having one.'

'Exactly,' Petra said. The red and gold lights from the street reflected in her eyes as she laughed. It was easy to see how Maratse had fallen for her.

'But he could be *romantic*?'

'*Aap*,' she said. 'In his own way.'

Petra ordered a second coffee and a slice of cake. I took out my notebook, drawing a curious smile from Petra as she looked at my antiquated note-taking equipment.

'That can't be cheap,' she said, nodding at my notebook.

'It wasn't,' I said. I pressed the nib of my pen to the page and waited for Petra to begin.

'It was Christmas,' she said. 'A long time ago. David had just sledged home with a broken tree and no duck.'

'No duck?'

'Actually, that's not right. It was no *partridge*. No bird for our Christmas Eve dinner.'

I must have frowned as I made a note. Petra laughed.

'I'd never tasted partridge,' she said. 'In fact, I don't think I ever have.'

'But Maratse tried to buy one?'

'A duck, yes, from the store.' Petra paused to take a bite of her cake, and then continued. 'He tried to buy it in Uummannaq, but that's not what the story is about.'

'He was supposed to be romantic,' I said, hoping I wouldn't offend Petra with my prompt.

'That's right,' she said. 'Here's what happened.'

Petra described a familiar scene, painting the houses with assorted colours, peeling the paint from the walls and the doors, placing cheeky ravens on the bitumen roofs and curious puppies on the deck. She described the deep, penetrating cold in the way that only people who have experienced it can – as a matter of fact, with an undertone of respect.

'You have to respect it,' she said. 'You certainly can't change it.'

I nodded, adding to and embellishing my notes until Petra was ready to continue.

Her story took us inside Maratse's house, the one he rented in Inussuk. I had never seen it, but I knew the type – a simple layout with two tiny rooms on the first floor. The stairs were steep, Petra remembered, and Maratse had struggled with them to begin with.

'He had a problem with his legs,' she said. 'But he never talked about it. No-one did.'

I waited for Petra to return to Maratse's house, which she did, describing the barest of furniture, a typical bachelor's pad that Petra was determined to change.

'It was nothing like my apartment. It was almost as if no-one lived there,' she said.

'Like a hunter's cabin?'

Petra nodded. 'Exactly like that, only less lived-in, if that is even possible.'

I had visited many cabins and huts in Greenland, together with Maratse. I knew what she meant, and could just picture the bare floors, the ash in front of the cast iron stove, and an array of rusty tins lined in a row on the shelf. Lived-in, where the dust collected in the furthest corners only, away from the living area centred around the stove where it was warmest.

'It was where he felt most comfortable,' Petra said. 'In a cabin. But it was a bit much that I had to live in one too.' She shrugged, and said, 'I'm a modern girl, I want modern things, and a bit of comfort. At least, more than just a dusty couch and a coffee table. That's not too much to ask. Is it?'

'No,' I said. The thought of Maratse's reaction made me smile, and I could just picture the conversation they must have had when Petra broached the subject of comfort and interior decorating. Luckily, she could remember the whole conversation.

'He took it well,' she said.

'With a grunt, perhaps?'

'*Aap*.'

That smile again, and the glitter of colour in her eyes.

'There were a few grunts,' she said. 'And five gold rings.'

The rings intrigued me, and I looked up as Petra described them.

'I suggested that he could at least find some Christmas decorations to hang up. I even borrowed one of those Christmas stars from Buuti.' Petra paused and the festive light in her eyes dulled for just a moment, as if the memory of Buuti or the memories associated with her were painful. 'I'm sorry,' she said. 'Buuti was very dear to me. She was Maratse's neighbour, the wife of his best friend.'

'Karl,' I said, surprising myself as I remembered the name.

'*Aap*,' Petra said. 'Anyway, the rings.' She pointed at a decoration behind me, and I turned to look at a golden mobile with stars hanging from different lengths of string attached to a ring hooked into the ceiling. 'It was something like that. He made it.'

'Out of gold rings?'

'Not quite,' Petra said, smiling for a moment before eating another forkful of cake. 'The tiny store in Inussuk didn't have much in the way of decorations, and after Maratse's disastrous trip into town for the bird and tree…'

'You didn't want to send him back again?'

'Would you?'

'No,' I said, although I could just picture Maratse's face as if Petra had suggested it.

'David went outside for a while – long enough for me to wonder if he had bumped into Karl. Which he had, but not in the way I thought. They weren't hiding, but when Buuti and I found them, you could see they had been up to something.'

'The rings?' I said, picturing the two Greenlanders making something in the shed.

Petra nodded. 'It had taken them the best part of an hour, about three metres of fishing line and the metal rings from five dog collars.'

'Metal? They weren't gold?'

'David tried to convince me that they were, but it was rust.' Petra rubbed her finger and thumb together. 'It flaked off between my fingers.'

'But this was the decoration?'

'Yes, and he and Karl hung it up in the living room. Buuti and I watched, too amused to criticise. We let them take their time, but really David was just stalling.'

'Stalling?'

'Either he was waiting for the right moment or building up courage. I don't know. But once the decoration was hanging from the ceiling, he took my hand and took the ring from my finger.'

'From another collar?' I asked, slightly confused.

'No,' she said. 'It was the ring he gave me after he sledged back from Uummannaq…'

'When he came back with the broken tree…'

'And a partridge.' Petra nodded. The soft Christmas light returned to her eyes with a renewed intensity. 'Maratse asked Karl and Buuti to sit on the sofa, then he took my hand and knelt down on one knee.' Petra brushed her fingers across her lips, then wiped at the tears, one from each eye, that trickled down her cheeks. 'He promised he would never leave me, that he would never let me go, that he would follow me wherever I led him, if only I would promise to stay with him forever.'

'He proposed,' I said.

'In his own simple way, yes.'

I waited for Petra to say more, but her gaze drifted back to the Christmas lights on the street, and then further, to the mountain tops, to the black winter sky and the Northern Lights twisting gently above Greenland.

THE END

The sixth day
of Christmas

~ Six geese a-laying ~

In which we meet Phyllis Frobisher who plays
a key role in *The Tapestry Bag* and *Lost Property*,
the first two novels in Isabella Muir's
Sussex Crime series, set in 1960s England.

Watching geese

~ Sussex, England, 1980 ~

There's a boat down by the river that has my name on it.

I won't sail in this boat, nor will I start the engine or navigate my way out to sea. But I'll travel in it nevertheless. Every night when I pull the eiderdown over my wrinkled body, close my eyes and drift off, I'll have the chance to journey to any place I choose. There will be daytime travels too. Each book I read will transport me to a new destination.

Early mornings as I wrap bony fingers around my mug of tea I will turn the pages of *Wuthering Heights* and let myself wander the Yorkshire moorlands with Cathy in search of her beloved Heathcliff. As dawn breaks the sun will shine onto the deck of my boat and I will lay one book down and pick up another.

This time I am transported to Thomas Hardy's Wessex to dance alongside Tess on the day she first sees Angel Clare. As the ribbons wind around the May pole, I thread ribbons through the edges of a pullover I have knitted that will keep me warm when the autumn arrives.

My plan is to celebrate my eightieth birthday on a houseboat. There are many who know me who think it is a fanciful idea. They want to hold a cosy afternoon tea party, offering plates of neatly cut sandwiches and iced fairy cakes to my friends.

Instead I will be on my boat. It's one I've had my eye on for some time. The painted wood has flaked away, the varnished deck is dull, the windows are yellow with mildew. I asked around and am told that its owner has passed away. His only surviving relative lives in a city, she has no interest in houseboats. I write to her, saying I would like to care for the boat, make it feel loved again.

My granddaughter, Libby, doesn't laugh when I tell her. Instead she asks me why.

'I have so much still to learn.' I try to explain.

'On a boat?'

'They say travel broadens the mind.'

'But you won't be going anywhere.'

'That's where you are wrong.'

She enlists the help of friends, more agile and able than me.

'Well, whatever your reasons, Gran, it sounds great,' she announces. Janie and Greg join the working party. I stand on the riverbank and watch them scrub and mop. It is when the fresh paint and varnish is complete that I know I have done the right thing.

All my life I have surrounded myself with books and yet for many years I didn't understand what the stories were trying to tell me. As a teacher, I encouraged my pupils to love the printed word. Some found it a struggle and yet they spoke proudly of other passions; to recognise the call of a nightingale, to take a piece of timber and fashion it into a table, to play a musical instrument and watch the sound transport someone to another place. These were gifts I didn't have and I know now that they are all equally as valid.

But for the first part of my life I was intolerant of anyone who wasn't like me, who didn't see the world through the same lens. For the last half of my life - for these past forty years I find I'm learning every day.

I was a teenager in the First World War, indignant and naive. I railed at my father when he gave permission to my brother to join the army. William was just eighteen. Just like thousands of others, my dear sweet brother never returned from the trenches. It was many years before I could forgive my father, when all the time I should have helped him through the grief that ate away at him. When I treated my father with disdain, with anger, I hadn't learned.

By the time it was all happening again I was nearly forty. Wiser, perhaps, but no less accepting. When I scolded a pupil who presented an empty homework book, explaining they had been helping their mother care for a newborn, I hadn't learned. My teaching duties were regularly interrupted by the bombing and for a time I lost my passion for words. They seemed so futile. Words hadn't stopped our country from going to war.

Now I am old I've let go of many things and replaced them with words again. I've learned to see things through the eyes of others. The people who are close to me teach me lessons every day. I find now that I am no longer the intolerant teacher, I have become the pupil.

My granddaughter, Libby, laughs her way through disappointments as though they are rain droplets, kept from touching her by the largest of all umbrellas. Janie negotiates a challenging path, trying to be a good wife and mother, while not losing herself in the process. Her father, Philip, tackles each day as though his two unseeing eyes give him all the vision he needs to navigate his life.

When my young friends have finished making my houseboat fresh and bright I will pack a few things into a suitcase and move into my new home. I have been watching from the sidelines, feeling guilty that I am not contributing to the industry that is turning an old wreck into something bold and gay. I spend time chatting to others who live on the water.

I discover there is a real community here. Many have lived in their floating home for years and have stories to tell. They speak with wonder in their voices as they describe how it is to wake in the morning to the sounds of moorhens and ducks, or gigantic carp banging on the hull, or of watching cormorants swoop for fish, or glimpsing a shy heron, still as a statue in the shadows. A woman, who will become my neighbour, introduces herself as Nell and goes on to recount the most wondrous sight; a flock of geese that took off from the riverbank just a foot away from her.

I've discovered that it's possible to travel through life from innocence to wisdom and I continue to learn through the printed word. New authors grab my attention, of course, but still the classics hold me in thrall. Modern writers offer me a chance to visit a time and place I have no wish to think of again. Stories of brave wartime deeds are reminders of events for which I need no reminding.

But some memories I grasp and cling onto. For each day of December I will choose a tale of Christmas. Some will bring reminders of childhood, my father reading *The little match girl* to me before he kissed me goodnight, with promises that I would never have to suffer as she did. Ebenezer Scrooge will whisper to me of ghosts of Christmas past, reminding me of the goodness that is there in all of us, even though it often needs to be tugged to the fore. And where will I travel to with these tales of Christmas? North, perhaps. To the land of Santa and reindeers, where elves are real and Rudolf always saves the day.

And my new neighbours will help me to continue learning. I will watch the geese take off from the riverbank and it will be the perfect birthday celebration.

THE END

The seventh day of Christmas

~ Seven swans a-swimming ~

In which we meet Detective Freja Hansen from *Blackout Ingénue*, the first full novel in Christoffer Petersen's Danish Crime series.

One of our swans is missing

~ Flensburg, Germany, 2019 ~

Detective Freja Hansen wiped the curry sauce from the front of her daughter's ski suit, and then brushed another spot from her cheek. Ayoe worked around her mother, chasing the slippery sausage slices around the paper tray with a wooden fork, leaning to one side, dipping her head as Freja wiped away the curry. Adam Hansen sipped his coffee, content to watch coloured Christmas lights reflecting on the faces of the two most important people in his life.

'Hold still, Ayoe,' Freja said.

'But the sausage is getting away.'

'And so is the curry sauce. You're covered in it.'

Adam laughed, and said, 'She really isn't Freja. Not yet anyway.' He turned his head to one side at the sound of geese honking from the closed-off area between the wooden market stalls.

'What's that, Daddy?'

'Geese,' he said.

'Geese?' Ayoe leaned backwards to get a better look. 'It's white,' she said. 'It looks like a swan.'

'Whoa, wait a second,' Freja said, catching Ayoe's arm. 'Currywurst, first. Geese and swans after.' She gave Adam one of those looks that he had learned to interpret as a *help needed but not received* look. He leaned across the table and pinched

Ayoe's paper tray between his finger and thumb, tugging it across the table.

'Let me help you, kiddo,' he said, taking Ayoe's fork.

Freja shook her head as Ayoe scooted off the bench and ran towards the goose enclosure. 'That wasn't quite what I meant,' she said.

'She was finished.' Adam frowned as the sausages proved to be just as elusive for him as they were for his daughter. He looked up as Ayoe ran back to the table; the sleeves of her ski suit shushed as she ran. 'What's up?' he asked, when he noticed her face.

'They've got them locked up,' Ayoe said. She looked at Freja. 'Behind bars, Mummy.'

'I'm sure it's just to keep them safe,' Freja said.

'No.' Ayoe shook her head. 'Not safe. There's a sign saying you have to guess the weight. If you guess right, you win the goose.'

'You can read German now?' Adam said. 'That's really good, Ayoe. I'm impressed.'

'It's in Danish, Dad,' she said, before turning back to Freja. 'You have to do something, Mummy.'

'We're in Germany, Sweetie. I'm not a police officer here,' she said. 'I'm sure they're fine.'

'But they're going to kill them,' Ayoe said.

Freja recognised the panic lines creasing her daughter's forehead and pulled her into a hug, sitting her on her knee as she tousled her hair.

'Do you remember what we talked about? You know where food comes from.'

'Yes,' Ayoe said. She twitched her head back towards the goose enclosure.

'Your sausage,' Freja said. 'That came from a pig.'

'We hope,' Adam said. The smile on his lips faded as Freja shot him a look.

'I know all this, Mummy. But a goose isn't a pig. It's a bird.'

'We eat duck at Christmas.'

'But they don't put the ducks in a pen and get people to chase them around and pick them up and then guess how much they weigh and…'

'Breathe, Baby,' Freja said.

'…and,' Ayoe said, with a short breath in which to breathe. 'They don't kill them and wrap them up for you to take home.'

'I'm sure they don't kill them here,' Freja said.

'But, Mummy, they do. It said so on the sign.'

Freja sighed. 'I just don't know what you want me to do, Sweetie.'

'Arrest them,' Ayoe said, pressing her palm to Freja's chest. 'You're a detective. You have to stop them.'

Freja leaned back a little to look at her daughter. 'What's got into you, Ayoe? Has something happened at school?'

'No.'

'Something you want to tell us about?' Freja shot a look at Adam, drawing him into the conversation.

'Are you worried about me, Ayoe? I'm fine. Everything is okay.'

'I know,' Ayoe said. 'It's just…' She didn't finish. Ayoe slipped off the bench and walked back towards the goose enclosure. Adam shook his head as Freja lifted her leg over the bench.

'Let her go, Freja.'

'Something's bothering her,' she said. 'It can't be the geese.' She pulled her smartphone from her pocket and opened the school app, scrolling through the list of lessons Ayoe had had during the week. 'Maybe there was a theme or something that's got her worked up.'

'A lot has happened recently,' Adam said. 'You were hurt in Scotland, then she was kidnapped…' He shrugged. 'She's got plenty to worry about. It doesn't have to be anything about school. If it's a reaction to something, well… I'm not sure what more we can do.' He nodded at the Christmas stalls. 'We're together, doing family things. We've established a routine, Freja. She's got a counsellor – a chance to talk about things. We've given her the stability that all the child psychologists talk about, and all the love she'll ever need and more.'

'I know, but…'

'But nothing,' he said. 'She's just reacting to something. It might even be the goose.'

'You're right.'

'If it is the goose, let it be the goose. Let's not make it something elsc unless we need to.'

Freja slipped her smartphone into her pocket. She smiled at Adam and then took his hand, turning to look for Ayoe as she squeezed his fingers. Freja leaned to one side to see around a family of four who were blocking her view of the goose enclosure. She frowned at the sound of a goose honking and hissing, followed by loud voices in German.

'Freja,' he said, as she tightened her grip.

'I can't see her.' She let go of Adam and swung her legs over the bench.

Freja weaved through the crowd of Christmas shoppers, the families, the older couples, and the tourists. Adam followed, pausing to tip the paper tray inside a wooden barrel lined with black plastic. He arrived at the goose enclosure a second or two after his wife.

'She's gone,' Freja said. 'I can't see her.'

'Let's give it a second,' Adam said. He pointed at the enclosure and at a German shouting and waving his hands. 'Something's going on.'

Freja focussed on the stall owner, stepping to one side as two German police officers worked their way through the crowds, calling for the man to calm down and stop shouting as they approached him.

'Someone has taken one of my geese,' the man said, raising his voice as the geese squawked at his feet.

'Freja,' Adam said, reaching for her arm as she took a step closer. 'Let them deal with it.'

She brushed his hand away and leaned close to the enclosure to better hear the exchange between the man and the police. Apparently, the goose was quite valuable.

'You want us to look for a goose?' the taller of the police officers asked.

'I want you to find the thief,' the man said.

Adam took a step closer to Freja, close enough to whisper in her ear as he gently gripped her by the arm. 'You know who the thief is, don't you?'

Freja nodded. 'Yes.'

'She can't be far.' Adam pointed at the geese. 'If it's even half the size of one of them...'

'Then they won't be difficult to spot,' Freja said. 'I'll go left.'

Adam pointed to the right. 'I'll see you on the other side.'

Ayoe might even have gotten away with it, Freja mused, if she had taken the smallest of the geese. But it seemed that the family trait of biting off more than one could chew and failing to learn from one experience to the next, ran strong in the Hansen family. The thought brought a tight smile to Freja's lips. It grew bigger, stretching across her mouth at the sound of a honk from behind one of the stalls, followed by a very Ayoe-like *shush*.

Adam walked around the stall, following the sound of the goose, and stopping to pick up a soft white feather. Freja pointed at a green canvas tarpaulin hooked around the back of a hot dog stand to hide the gas cylinders. She nodded and pointed. Adam mouthed, 'I'll wait here.'

Another honk from the goose and a *shush* from Ayoe masked Freja's footsteps as she approached the tarpaulin. Freja knelt and lifted one end, peering beneath it as she looked at her daughter tucked between the gas cylinders, one arm tucked tightly around the goose's back and wing, as she wrested her other hand around the goose's beak.

'Do you need any help, Sweetie?'

Ayoe looked at her mother, her face flushing with a mix of exertion and embarrassment. 'They were going to kill him, Mummy,' she said.

'Only if someone guessed the weight,' she said. 'Did you see anyone pick it up?'

'No.'

'That's because there was another sign telling people not to touch the geese.' Freja shrugged. 'It makes it hard to guess the weight, don't you think?'

Ayoe frowned, as if she hadn't thought about that.

Freja pointed at the goose squirming within Ayoe's tiny hands, and said, 'How much do you think it weighs?'

Ayoe paused for a moment, struggling as the goose made another attempt to flap out of her grasp. 'I don't know,' she said. 'A lot, maybe.'

'Maybe?' Freja nodded. 'How about we let Daddy take the goose back and you and I can go and find some honey cakes for Granddad?'

Ayoe nodded. She waited for Adam to reach in and take the goose from her arms, before taking her mother's hand. Freja pulled Ayoe out from between the two gas cylinders. She brushed the feathers from Ayoe's ski suit, and then pulled Ayoe close, wrapping her arm around her. Ayoe fidgeted as they watched Adam struggle with the goose all the way back to the enclosure.

'Are you going to arrest me, Mummy?'

'Yep,' Freja said.

'Really?'

'I was thinking about it. But…'

'But what?'

'Well, if your daddy can guess how much you weigh, then I think we'll just take you home instead.' Freja brushed her daughter's hair and kissed her forehead. 'What do you think about that?'

Ayoe leaned into Freja's side, pressing her head against her mother's ribs as she held her hand. 'That's all right,' she said. 'But you'll whisper it to him if he gets it wrong, won't you, Mummy.'

'That's called cheating, Ayoe,' Freja said.

'The same as the man with the goose, then,' Ayoe said.

'Yes. I suppose you're right.'

They said nothing more until Adam returned, smiling as he plucked the last feathers from the seams and zipper of his jacket. Freja pulled him close, kissed his cheek and whispered in his ear. Adam frowned as he looked at Ayoe. He shook his head for a moment, and then took her hand.

'I don't know, Ayoe,' he said, as she stared up at him. 'That's an awful lot of kilos for one goose.'

THE END

The eighth day
of Christmas

~ Eight maids a-milking ~

In which we meet Walter, Patrick and Anna from
Isabella Muir's novel *The Forgotten Children*.

Lot 8: The milkmaid

~ Anglesey, Wales, 1990 ~

With just three weeks to go until Christmas it was rare for all three of them to have a morning off. For Walter and Patrick that Friday morning represented a brief respite between completing the fencing of the lower paddock and starting on the shearing. Patrick was well practised at handling the sheep, holding each one still while he ran the shears around its body, always attempting to achieve the perfect fleece. Sometimes he managed it.

Since they had been working together he had often challenged Walter to a time trial. But it was always in good humour and whoever won (usually Patrick) they would laugh about it.

When the brothers knew they could slip away for a few hours that Friday morning they told Anna.

'See if you can get the morning off. We can spend a few hours in town together. Your choice as to what we do, where we go.'

The shop manager agreed, telling Anna that she deserved it. Since she had been working at the wool shop in town takings had increased. When she found the job back at the beginning of the summer, it was the cause of more laughter from the brothers.

'We should cut out the middleman,' Walter said. 'If you learned to spin the fleece we could sell the wool direct from the farm.'

Although it was said in jest the idea sat with Anna and often, in her quiet moments, she played with colours in her mind. In her lunch hour she visited the local library, read all she could about natural dyes. One day perhaps. She was grateful for the job, her wages meant she contributed to their life together. The three of them as equals.

It seemed that the wool shop customers valued her, they asked for her opinion, showing her their knitting patterns, asking for advice about the best yarn to use, what to do when the tension square was too large or too small. She made sure she always had a project of her own on the go, a cardigan or jumper. Over the months since starting in the shop she had completed an Aran sweater for Patrick and a Fair Isle jumper for Walter. Both patterns were complex; she found that the more challenging the design the more she enjoyed it. It was a compliment to her that they wore them every day through one of the harshest winters to hit Anglesey in several years. It was a comforting thought that her hands had created something to keep them protected and warm, as though she was there when they tended the animals or ploughed the fields, wrapping her arms around each of them.

But that Friday morning she had another project in mind. Each time she had passed the auction house on her way to work she noticed a photograph on display. It had been chosen as the image for the front cover of the auction catalogue. It was a patchwork quilt by Kaffe Fassett. Even as she looked at the small photograph, she was so intoxicated by the vibrancy of the colours that it was as though she was having a psychedelic experience. (Not that she had ever experimented with LSD, but she had read enough about its effects to guess what it would be like.)

She had first seen the designer's work discussed in a knitwear magazine. Another trip to the library enabled her to read more about him. Born in California, Fassett started to make his name when he joined forces with the Scottish fashion designer, Bill Gibb. Fassett had developed an extraordinary approach to colour, which he maximised in the way he worked with fabrics, knitwear, needlepoint and patchwork. He had even applied his imaginative ideas to paintings and mosaics. His work was to be the subject of an exhibition at the Victoria and Albert Museum in London. It would be the first time a living textile artist had such a show.

Of course, she wanted to be there. She dreamed of wandering through the museum, gazing at the wondrous pieces of tapestry and needlecraft. She wondered how long she would have to stare at each piece before it was so closely stamped on her memory that she would only have to close her eyes and she could re-imagine it in all its fine detail.

As she sat beside Walter and Patrick in the auction house that Friday morning she found that she was almost holding her breath for the moment that the patchwork quilt would be held aloft as the auctioneer started the bidding. She had told the boys briefly about Kaffe Fassett, but held back from telling them about her dream. The money it would take to travel to London, stay overnight, would be enough to keep them in food for the week. Besides, her real desire was not merely to look at Fassett's work, but to emulate him. And that nugget of truth would surely result in laughter from them both.

The auctioneer was working swiftly through the lots. While there were fifty or more people attending the auction, very few of them were bidding. Anna's guess was that the main attraction of the event, which was taking place on a cold, wet Friday morning, was the warmth of the venue. It was evidently too warm for Walter and Patrick, who spent most of their days outdoors on the farm. Whenever she turned to look at them one or other was wiping sweat from his forehead. Fortunately they had not chosen their hand-knitted sweaters to wear that day.

'Interesting choice for your morning off,' Patrick commented when she explained her rationale for wanting to go to the auction. 'A bit of a busman's holiday, isn't it?'

Walter had said little, but then that was Walter's way. He only spoke when he felt he had something worthwhile to say.

'There's a chance I'll be able to see the quilt up close.'

'You'll not be bidding on it though,' Patrick teased.

The first few lots held little interest for any of them. A Victorian stool; a porcelain teapot that was supposed to date back to the Chinese Ming dynasty (Anna had her doubts); and an assortment of carpenter's tools that looked as though they had spent the last fifty years in someone's shed.

'Lot 8, The Milkmaid, by Johannes Vermeer,' the auctioneer announced.

The audience fell silent. Those who had previously been coughing at inappropriate moments, or chattering loud enough to make the bids difficult to hear, now ceased their interruptions. It was as though everyone was holding a collective breath. They turned, almost as one, to look at the painting, which was being held up by the auctioneer's assistant.

'I don't understand,' Anna whispered. 'How can a seventeenth century masterpiece be for sale in an auction house in Anglesey. It must be worth millions.'

'It's just a painting,' Walter said.

'A priceless painting,' Anna countered.

There was a rustling among the crowd, as people started leafing through the catalogue.

'What does it say about it?' Patrick was more fascinated by the reaction to the painting, than by the painting itself. It was nice enough, but quite drab, in his opinion. The milkmaid looked sad, as though her life was little more than drudgery. She was depicted pouring milk from a jug into a bowl, with the only other fare on the table being a rough hunk of bread.

'Perhaps she is making bread pudding,' Walter said, sensing his brother's disenchantment with the image. 'It could be that she is happy in her work, not sad, but focused.'

It was then that the auctioneer cleared his throat, tapped the gavel on the table, not to denote a successful bid, but to gain everyone's attention.

'Ladies and gentlemen. You will see in your catalogue that this is, of course, a copy of the original painting. It would be foolish to imagine we might have the real Vermeer here in our humble auction house.' He finished his statement with a chuckle.

'A bit of a trick, eh? Just to see if everyone's awake,' Patrick said.

Anna's mind had moved on. She was no longer thinking about the authenticity of the painting, but about the ability of one person to copy the work of another, with such success that it was as if those looking on were gazing at the real thing.

'It is a form of sharing,' Walter said.

Patrick and Anna turned towards him, each waiting for further explanation.

'One painting in a museum in Amsterdam can be enjoyed by all those people who are able to visit Amsterdam. Multiply that experience by creating copies, then lots of people can enjoy the same thing.'

'But it's not the same thing, is it? It's a copy.' Anna couldn't decide if the emotions she was experiencing were of annoyance, or something else.

They fell silent for a while. The copy of the Vermeer fetched a little over one hundred pounds. Mutterings among the audience suggested that most felt it was a poor copy, an amateur's attempt and that the frame of the painting was worth more than the image itself.

'Lot 12, patchwork quilt by Kaffe Fassett,' the auctioneer said.

'Not a copy this time though, eh?' a member of the audience quipped.

Anna got up from her seat and moved forward to be as close as possible to the item that was being held up for everyone to see. She had never in her life seen anything more beautiful. Every square depicted a different flower, the overall hues being every shade from vermilion, through russet, to the palest pinks and greens. It was like stepping into a garden when the most vibrant colours were in full bloom, all at the same moment. She couldn't bear to turn away from it, she was entranced. So much so that she didn't even hear the bids and moments later the quilt had been folded away and the next lot was being held aloft.

As she returned to her seat she felt a ridiculous need to cry. She took a handkerchief from her jacket pocket and pretended she was about to sneeze, blowing her nose and wiping her face, hoping that Walter and Patrick hadn't noticed.

'You don't need to buy someone else's vision,' Walter said.

She turned to him, forcing a smile, before remembering that Walter understood emotions more than anyone she had ever met.

'You can create your own,' he said. 'You will create your own.'

As she sat between the brothers, each held a hand out to take hers. This time it was as though they were wrapping their arms around her, offering warmth and protection.

She closed her eyes and colours danced behind her eyelids.

THE END

The ninth day
of Christmas

~ Nine ladies dancing ~

In which we meet Emma Østergård from
Paint the Devil and *Lost in the Woods*, the first two
books in Christoffer Petersen's Wolf Crimes
series set in Denmark and Alaska.

Nine to five and dancing

~ Copenhagen, Denmark, 2020 ~

Emma Østergård is tucked into the alcove she has built within her room. She doesn't see the cheap red, green and blue party lights reflecting off the walls of the living room, they are hidden from view. The alcove is courtesy of IKEA, the Swedish furniture shop. A desk and, on either side, bookshelves she has built herself, pushed sideways against the wall. The shelves on the left of the desk hold her favourites, the wolf books, both scientific and sociological. Some of them belong to her father, although he is unlikely to ever get them back. The edges are worn, as are the covers. Worn away from turning the pages over and over again. To her right are the heavier biology books. She tugs at the base of the thick spines to pull one of them onto the desk. Pushing her fingers through her long, dark fringe, she rests her elbow on the desk, and opens the book. There is plenty to occupy her here, she can supplement the dry and factual predator prey relationships – those in the books to her right – with observations from the field, and those in her head. Emma's head dances with wolves and she has forgotten all about Christmas.

'Not again,' Pernille says, as she enters Emma's room. 'You promised.'

'I just have to finish this. It's important.'

'It's Christmas. Nine to five means you stop work at five. You stop studying, reading, or whatever else you are working on.' Pernille pads across the room in her bare feet. She twirls, crackling the taffeta hems of her long, red dress – thin straps over bare shoulders. 'That's right, Em,' Pernille says, as Emma bites her bottom lip. 'It's tonight.'

'I'm so sorry, P. I forgot.'

'No, you didn't.'

'Honestly, this time I did.'

'This time?'

'The last time, well, I didn't forget.'

Pernille smooths the hems of her dress and pretends not to hear Emma. She walks over to Emma's cupboard, opens the door and roots inside, searching for a dress among what she calls Emma's *practical clothes*.

'Linus is coming tonight. You remember him, Em? The Norwegian?'

'Yes, of course. Linus.'

'He's a biology student too, just like you.'

'I know.'

'He's had several classes with your dad.'

Yes, Emma thinks. *Lots of people have.*

'But he doesn't hold it against you.' Pernille reaches into the cupboard and pulls out Emma's dress. She pokes her head between the straps and lets the hanger hang on the back of her neck. 'This one, Em,' she says.

'It's the only dress I have.'

'Which is why I think it should be this one.' Pernille swishes the dress as she dances towards

Emma. She pokes at Emma's bare arms and tugs at the black vest she is wearing on top of her sweatpants. 'This outfit might be *en vogue* for bright young biologists at the University of Copenhagen, but I think Linus would prefer the dress. Especially for dancing.'

Emma sighs. 'I'm not ready, P. I don't know that I will ever be ready.'

'Because of Jacob?'

'Yes.'

'Even now, after all this time?'

'Yes, even now.'

Pernille sits down on the edge of Emma's bed, tucking Emma's dress onto her lap. She looks at her flatmate, studies her for a moment, looks into Emma's clear blue eyes set in a pale face framed with her dark brown, almost black hair. She knows Emma has experienced trauma, but it's as if she is blanking out her memories, choosing to lose herself in her wolf studies. 'When did you last see your therapist?'

'I was there recently,' Emma says, glancing to one side.

'How recently? Last week, or last month?'

'The second one, maybe.'

Pernille lays Emma's dress flat on the bed, before standing up.

'And you're not coming?' she says.

'I don't think so.'

'Not even if Linus is going to be there?'

Emma shakes her head. 'I'm just not ready. Not yet.'

'What if I told you he was a lupin?'

'A what?' Emma frowns.

'You know, a man who turns into a wolf.'

Emma's frown fades and her eyes light up as she laughs. 'You mean *Lycan*. A lupin is a flower.'

'Which is why I'm studying mathematics, with clean nails, and you're grubbing around in the dirt looking for wolf shit.'

'What can I say, P? It makes me happy.'

'It makes you weird,' Pernille says. She takes two steps and flings her arms around Emma's neck.

'You smell good, P.'

'I know. It's for the Lycans!' Pernille lets go of Emma and walks to the door and stops. A sad smile creeps slowly onto her lips as she looks back at Emma. 'I worry, you know.'

'I know.' Emma says.

'I'll leave you to it, then.'

'Thanks.' Emma waits until Pernille is gone before turning back to her studies.

She doesn't hear the traffic on the street, or the burst of Christmas pop music as the neighbours play their after pub quiz. She's lost in the words of L. David Mech as he tracked wolves across Ellesmere Island, breaking dry spore into two halves to study the contents. Emma leans into the words. She walks alongside the wolf biologist, if only in her mind. She hears the howls of a wolf pack, stops when he stops, nods that she has heard it, before realising she did hear it, and that it wasn't in her mind.

Emma looks up from the book and leans back in her chair. She hears another howl, long and mournful. The rational part of her brain reminds her that the Danish wolves are in Jutland, predominantly on the west coast, not in the capital.

'So it's a recording,' she says, quietly, as she pushes back her chair.

Emma pads to the door of her room and into the living area of their tiny student apartment. She stops at another howl. She crosses to the window that looks down onto the communal courtyard at the rear of the apartment blocks. Someone has strung party lights in a low-hanging cross between the bike sheds. The coloured lights reflect in the puddles of December rain that collect in the dips and holes of the asphalt courtyard.

Another howl draws Emma all the way to the apartment door. She pulls her sneakers over her bare feet and grabs her father's winter jacket, zipping it to her chin as she jogs down the stairs, one flight, to the back door.

A fourth howl carries her through the door and into the courtyard. The fifth howl is drowned by soft laughter and the clink of glass beer bottles and mixers.

'Emma Østergård,' Pernille says, as she steps out of the shadow of the bicycle shed. 'You are a predictable tramp, but I love you.'

'It was you?' Emma says, shaking her head as Pernille steps into the light.

'I found the wolves on YouTube,' she says. 'And I found these lovely people at the ball.' Pernille reaches into the shadows and waves people out of them; a few girls Emma recognises from her year, and a tall, blond Norwegian who looks surprisingly good in a tuxedo. 'The ball was boring without you,' Pernille says, taking the

Bluetooth speaker from Linus' hands, before giving him a gentle push towards Emma.

'We know each other,' Linus says, as he reaches for Emma's hand.

'Yes,' she whispers.

'We like each other. That's what Pernille says.'

'Yes…'

Emma's heart begins to beat faster, as if she is chasing Arctic hares across the tundra, together with the pack. But the Alpha female snaps at her, spoiling her trajectory, and pushing her off course, off the tundra, out of the Arctic and into the arms of the tall, blond Norwegian, and she is dancing, in the courtyard, among friends, and, for the moment at least, far, far away from wolves.

THE END

The tenth day of Christmas

~ Ten lords a-leaping ~

In which we meet Hugh Furness from *Lost Property*, the second novel from Isabella Muir's Sussex Crime series, set in 1960s England.

Lords

~ Sussex, England, 1968 ~

I'm on my way to the local pub, where I plan to spend this Friday evening. I've never spent an evening on my own in a pub, but each week I'm trying new experiences.

At the beginning of the week I decided to teach myself how to make cottage pie. I followed a recipe - I might add that it was with great success. The only part of the recipe I didn't notice, until it was too late, was that the ingredients were intended to make enough for four people. As a consequence I enjoyed cottage pie every evening from Monday until Thursday.

I made the experience more interesting by keeping a notebook beside me on the dining table, and marking down a score. I gave the dish six out of ten on the first night. On subsequent nights the flavour improved. By Wednesday the minced beef had taken on the flavour of the Oxo and gravy browning, such that I scored it an eight. Unfortunately, for the last evening my supper was a disappointment. Reheating the meal on so many occasions, even though I'd added extra gravy each time, had resulted in the potato topping becoming dry and uninviting.

Now that Friday has arrived I will go to the pub early enough to have my supper there. Steak and kidney pie, perhaps, or sausages. Providing cottage pie is not the only dish on the menu, I should be fine.

These last months have been as difficult as I thought they would be. The level of my grief didn't surprise me, but perhaps my response to it did, just a little. At first I found it impossible to sleep. I would lay on my back in our double bed, staring at the ceiling, forcing myself not to turn onto my left side. I knew that as soon as I turned and saw the empty space beside me it would be as though I had been kicked in the stomach. I would need to bring my knees up and clench them to me to ease the pain.

After weeks of sleepless nights, of pacing the rooms downstairs in the early hours, longing for the dawn to break, everything changed. The nights that followed saw me falling into a deep sleep as soon as I climbed into bed, pulling the bedspread right up to my chin. And eight, sometimes ten hours later I would wake, glance at my bedside clock, turn onto my right side and doze off again. Why get up? What was there that needed to be done?

On the day a neighbour knocked on my front door I knew things had gone too far. I invited her in and only then did I see my home through her eyes. The kitchen sink piled high with dirty dishes, empty cups left on the floor beside the sofa, clothes thrown over the backs of chairs. For the first time I smelled the stale air, my own staleness.

'Well Mr Furness, let's get you tidied up, shall we?' she said and set about cleaning and returning my home to order.

At first I watched, thinking only, *This isn't who I am. This isn't the RAF pilot Winifred married, whose life was based on order and discipline.* I began to form the words for an apology. But it wasn't an apology that was needed. Instead I joined her in the sweeping and polishing duties, drying the dishes that she washed, putting them back into their rightful places.

A couple of hours later I left her to make us both a pot of tea, while I went upstairs and had a bath, returning in a clean, but crumpled shirt and the one remaining pair of trousers that were still presentable.

I made a promise to myself that day that I would honour Winnie's memory by attempting something new each week. These new experiences would force me to look forward, into what until then had felt like an abyss.

With the summer months encouraging me outdoors I decided to spend the day at Lords Cricket Ground. Even as I pressed my trousers, selected a fresh shirt and my best linen jacket, I could imagine Winnie laughing. I'd taken a mild interest in the sport over the years and frequently tried to explain the rules to her. In between fits of giggles, she tried to repeat my explanation back to me, *'They're in, then they're out. It seems very confusing to me. Innings and outings, silly mid-off and golden ducks. It's like a whole other language.'* Nevertheless, she listened patiently when the test match came on the wireless, asking for guidance as to who might be winning, as the scoring still defeated her.

It was with these thoughts that I made the train journey into London, caught the Underground and arrived, along with many others, at the ground described as the 'home of cricket'. A new stand had been completed and it was there I took my place, watching the Second Test, England against Australia. I wanted England to win, of course I did. But my focus wasn't the success or failure of the batsmen and bowlers; it was my attempt to clear my mind of all the anxiety that had been building since I found Winnie's diary.

It was after I had helped my neighbour to put my home in order, that I felt brave enough to start sorting through Winnie's belongings. The hardest part was handling each item of clothing that still smelled of her. Each Christmas I would buy her a bottle of *L'aimant* by Coty and it was this perfume that pervaded the silks and satins, the wool and linen. It was as if I was holding the very essence of her each time I took an item, folded it neatly and put it into a bag, ready to pass it on to someone less fortunate.

I thought about the nature of fortune. Many couples who met when we did, in the middle of the bloodiest years of the Second World War, didn't even make it to the altar. One or other would fall foul of the fighting, through gunfire or bombing. A pilot may be shot down, but just as easily a civilian may be crushed under the falling debris of their home, while they are doing nothing more than preparing supper. We survived those years and for that I am eternally grateful.

I sorted through all her clothes, but there was one item I couldn't dispose of. Her rose-coloured coat. The coat she wore the first time I met her. The coat that would feature in another story, a tale of bitter recriminations, secrets and lies. But that is not for now. For now I will gain pleasure from opening the wardrobe door from time to time and imagine my Winnie wearing the coat, just as if she is still here with me.

With her clothes tidied away, I made a start on the rest. Her sewing basket, where I found a pair of my socks, partly darned. A cloth bag filled with curlers and scarves. A leather vanity case with powder and lipsticks. And then I moved on to her diaries. She kept one for each year that we were together. It was when the press cutting fell from the diary for the year of 1946 that I realised she had known all along. Each of us wanting to protect the other from a secret that could have broken us both and may still break me.

It's strange to think that as an RAF pilot I confronted danger every day, flying low into enemy territory, knowing each time I took off from the airstrip that I may never return. And yet the discovery of the press cutting made me realise that it was now time to ask questions and listen to answers that may frighten me more than all I have experienced before.

And so, my day at Lords Cricket Ground, formed the perfect distraction. It seems I am a coward after all.

Since my visit to Lords I have attended several events organised by our local community. Talks on gardening, Anglo-Saxon history, even one explaining the intricacies of the stock market. By playing chess regularly I find that I am improving my game, although more and more the persistent cough that troubles me day and night becomes an irritant. Not just to me, but to any and all of my chess partners.

Each day that passes, the voices in my head remind me that I have to stop prevaricating. And now, as I walk to the pub, the voices are so loud that I know I can no longer ignore them.

THE END

The eleventh day of Christmas

~ Eleven pipers piping ~

In which we meet a young David Maratse – Qilingatsaq, and his grandfather, Equ. Many of Maratse's childhood adventures are recalled in the series of novellas starting with *Katabatic*.

The piebald piper

~ Ittoqqortoormiit, Greenland, 1986 ~

Qilingatsaq watched his grandfather slip his feet inside the polar bear skin trousers. He lifted his head as Equ stood up, watched him slip his arms inside the straps that held the heavy trousers up, before slipping his feet inside a worn but warm pair of sealskin *kamikker*. Equ sat down and beckoned for Qilingatsaq to cross the kitchen floor and join him.

'Where are your skin trousers, Qilingatsaq?' Equ asked, as he tugged at the threadbare jogging trousers the young Maratse wore.

'I don't have any, *ata*.'

Equ pointed to the utility room beside the kitchen, and said, 'Look in the cupboard.'

Qilingatsaq padded into the utility room, clambered over and around the litter of shoes and boots until he reached the cupboard. The door swung wide open when he tugged at the handle, and his eyes widened when he saw the child-sized pair of polar bear skin trousers hanging on a wooden hanger. He reached up to unhook the trousers, removed them from the hanger and then clamped them to his chest as he made his way back to the kitchen. The polar bear hairs tickled Qilingatsaq's nose as he pressed his face into them.

'*Juullimi pilluarit*,' Equ said, tousling Qilingatsaq's hair as he leaned against him. 'Now put them on, we have work to do.'

Qilingatsaq slipped his thin legs inside the skin trousers while Equ helped him adjust the straps. He smoothed his small hands through the thick hairs, before running into the utility room to take his *kamikker* down from the line stretched across the room and tied to the metal water pipes. Qilingatsaq used a broom handle to knock his *kamikker* onto the floor. He let the broom clatter and slide along the wall as he slipped his feet inside the sealskin shoes. Equ joined him in the utility room and they both pulled on winter coats before stepping outside.

'*Ata*,' Qilingatsaq said, as they walked down corridors of deep snow. 'Where are we going?'

'You'll see,' Equ said, and then nothing more until the path stopped at a snow staircase leading up and onto the rocks beside their house. Equ pointed and waited for Qilingatsaq to climb the steps. 'Do you remember the bitch with pups?' he said, as he caught his breath at the top of the steps.

'*Iiji.*'

Equ smiled, and said, 'Come and see.'

Qilingatsaq's eyes lit up as he caught the first snuffles of the young sledge dog puppies. He smelled them a second later – a mix of sour socks and sawdust. He picked up one of the puppies, feeling its warm and slick body in his hands as he reached inside the doghouse, only to let it go when its mother twitched beside him.

'Wait for it,' Equ said. He pointed at a tiny white puppy with chocolate and black patches on his head and rump.

The puppy opened its mouth wide, then closed it. Wide again. Then closed.

'It can't breathe,' Qilingatsaq said.

'It's okay,' Equ said. 'It's not trying to breathe; it's trying to sing.'

'It wants to sing?'

'*Imaqa*,' Equ said. 'Maybe.' He tugged Qilingatsaq's arm and they moved away from the doghouse. 'Are your trousers warm?' he asked.

'*Iiji.*'

'You feel like a hunter now, eh?'

'I am a hunter, *ata.*'

'Good,' Equ said. 'And hunters must look after their dogs.'

'*Iiji.*'

'These are your dogs now, Qilingatsaq. Will you look after them, like a hunter looks after his dogs?'

'*Iiji.*'

'Every day, even on Christmas Eve?'

'I will, *ata.*'

'Good.' Equ pointed at the piebald pup, and said, 'He is the smallest. You need to keep a special eye on him.'

Qilingatsaq nodded, as he knelt in the snow in front of the doghouse.

'And you will come in when you are cold?'

'*Iiji.*'

Equ left Qilingatsaq with the puppies as he organised the food for the team he had anchored down on the ice. Qilingatsaq was still with the pups when he returned forty minutes later. He didn't move when Equ called that it was time to come and eat. And only when Equ came to fetch him, did Qilingatsaq look up.

'Your fingers are turning blue, Qilingatsaq. You must come inside.'

'Not yet, *ata*,' he said.

'No?' Equ knelt beside his grandson. 'Why not?'

'I'm waiting for my piper to sing.'

THE END

The twelfth day
of Christmas

~ Twelve drummers drumming ~

In which we meet Philip Chandler, the father of
Janie Juke, from Isabella Muir's Sussex Crime
series, including *The Tapestry Bag*, *Lost Property*, and
The Invisible Case, all three of which are set in
1960s England.

The drummer boy

~ Italy, 1946 ~

When I was twelve and thirsty for knowledge, my father sent me off to the library. There I spent hours poring over history books. I read the stories of past civilisations and learned about lost traditions. The people of Ancient Egypt believed that turning your shoes upside down would displease the Gods. Showing dirty soles to the deities who lived above would bring bad luck. The Ancient Greeks had their own superstitions and as a young boy I thought it amusing when I discovered they believed that spitting was a way to chase the devil away. Unfortunately I didn't avoid a clip round the ear when I was caught following Greek tradition, despite my protests that I was merely trying to ensure good luck would follow me.

But it was the tradition of the drummer boy that really captured my imagination. I read about a seven-year-old boy who led soldiers into battle during the American War of Independence, banging his drum, announcing to the enemy that an attack was imminent. An attack that would surely lead to his death. I read of other drummer boys, all around my age, who (according to the history books) were proud to be a mascot for the troops. I spoke to my father about it.

'It was different then,' was his response. 'People were different then.'

'But they must have known they were going to die.'

'There was always the hope they would be on the winning side.'

And now, years later, I understand a little more about hope.

Today is the first day of Advent, a time to look forward. Anticipation. No one knows what lies ahead, but perhaps it's enough to hope. As I stand looking out to sea, my hope is that one day the fishing boats will return to this harbour. This natural inlet has seen only bloody conflict for too long and now deserves a gentler future.

For years life has been all about running, towards the enemy, or with fear in the opposite direction. But now as I walk I close my eyes to the rubble, the damaged buildings and blood-stained streets. The cessation of conflict came almost six years after it had all begun. Back then at the start, on a warm September day in Sussex, I believed like many others that it would all be over by Christmas. We didn't know then that six Christmases would pass before the bombs and the bodies stopped falling. Too many bodies, too many bombs.

Now with the silence comes an emptiness, but also the anticipation of what is to come.

I am reminded of childhood Christmases. The hush of those hours before midnight mass when Mother would make me lay on the sofa, tell me to close my eyes. *Try to sleep a little.* She should have remembered from her own childhood days that the imaginings of what was to come was as fuel to a fire, sending sparks in all directions. Each time I tried to close my eyes they popped open again of their own accord, like the Jack-in-the-box I was given for my eighth birthday.

But I was an obedient child. I lay as still as my excitement would allow and listened to the whispers filtering through from the kitchen. That night before Christmas was all about preparation. Peeling vegetables for a dinner of abundance, rolling out pastry to be filled with sweet currants, raisins and mixed spice. Hidden preparations involving wrapping paper, long woollen socks stuffed with oranges and nuts.

Today, as I walk beside the broken harbour, I'm anticipating something else. Not gifts, not scent-filled sweetmeats, but a moment during which I will make a decision.

A man ahead of me raises a hand in friendship. Two years ago that hand would have held a gun, its barrel trained on me, the enemy. During times of conflict we obey orders. We don't get to choose. Our commanding officer says *'Fire'* and we do so, without thought or hesitation.

But now I can make my own choices. The decision facing me appears simple and yet is more difficult than any choice made so far in the twenty years I have lived. I can join my comrades and return home to England, or I can remain here in Italy and discover what it is to be a foreigner in a foreign land.

Back home my mother is waiting. My father too, although he would never admit to it. Mother's letters have been filled with nothingness, a normality that kept me going when there was nothing normal to grab onto. If I return she will greet me at our front door, pull me inside, feed me hot, buttered crumpets and brush away any talk of darkness.

If I stay here there will be new traditions to make. I've been told that Italian families sit up all through the night of Christmas Eve, playing cards, telling stories. There are no secret whisperings over mince pie making, no pigs in blankets, or plum pudding to anticipate. Instead the old, gnarled fingers of the *nonnas* prepare the hand-made pasta, following recipes handed down from their mother and many mothers before her. The little parcels of pasta are stuffed with love and memories.

It's a gamble, but then I've been gambling every day since I enlisted.

'My name is Philip Chandler,' I told the sergeant at the army recruitment centre.

'And you're ready to join up, are you lad? Ready to be killed?'

Two questions that I wasn't prepared for, the answer to one inevitably becoming the answer to the other.

But the war is done and I'm alive. Now my gamble takes a different form. If I stay here in this country of light and warmth, it will take time before I'm accepted, before I am on the inside looking out, linking arms with my Italian brothers. Roll forward five years, maybe ten.

Some of my fellow soldiers have met pretty Italian women, gathered them up and swept them north, to Britain. Their future is set, the rolling of pasta will give way to the rolling of pastry, the light and warmth replaced for much of the time by cold and grey. But it's an easy choice to make when love is driving it.

So here is my gamble, a throw of the dice, a toss of a coin. I know which way I want it to fall.

It's Advent. I'm looking forward. I am the drummer boy who has survived. One day the fishing boats will return to this harbour. I'll stand on the quayside, watch the fishermen haul in their catch. I'll walk beside the turquoise Mediterranean sea, before sitting outside a *trattoria*. In my perfect Italian I will order *spaghetti alla vongole*, anticipating the sweet scent of the clams. Then on Christmas Eve, as I deal a hand of cards, I will tell my child about the English traditions of a stuffed bird and Brussels sprouts and he or she will laugh in disbelief.

THE END

About the authors

Isabella Muir is the author of a popular crime series – the *Sussex Crime Mysteries*. The stories are set in the 1960s and feature a young librarian and amateur sleuth, Janie Juke, who has a passion for Agatha Christie. All that Janie has learned from her hero, Hercule Poirot, she is able to put into action as she sets off to solve a series of crimes and mysteries.

Isabella's latest novel – *The Forgotten Children* – takes her writing into another genre. Still focusing on events in the 1960s, *The Forgotten Children* tells the story of the injustices experienced by thousands as a result of the British child migrant policy.

And if you have enjoyed these short stories, then you might like to dip into Isabella Muir's short story anthology, *Ivory Vellum*, or take a peek at her Sussex Crime novellas – *Divided we Fall* and *More than Ashes*.

You can discover more about **Isabella's** books and characters on her website, or download a free short story when you sign up for Isabella Muir's newsletter.

www.isabellamuir.com

About the authors

Christoffer Petersen writes crime novels and thrillers set in Greenland, Scandinavia and the Arctic. His most popular character to date is retired police constable David Maratse. Maratse first appeared as a supporting character in *The Ice Star*, and has since appeared as the main character in four novels and fourteen novellas. He makes a cameo appearance in other novels including *The Calendar Man*, the first full novel to feature police commissioner Petra 'Piitalaat' Jensen.

You can discover more about **Christoffer's** books and characters on his website, or download a free short story when you sign up for Christoffer Petersen's newsletter.

www.christoffer-petersen.com

Printed in Great Britain
by Amazon